P9-DFS-215

WANTED: BEST FRIEND

by A. M. Monson
pictures by Lynn Munsinger

Dial Books for Young Readers New York

Sandy Hook School
Library Media Center
Sandy Hook, CT 06482

E
MON
C-1

To M.H.
For oatmeal, wonderful notes, and all the rest...
A. M. M.

For James

L. M.

Published by Dial Books for Young Readers
A Division of Penguin Books USA Inc.
375 Hudson Street
New York, New York 10014

Text copyright © 1997 by Ann M. Monson
Pictures copyright © 1997 by Lynn Munsinger
All rights reserved
Designed by Ann Finnell
Printed in Hong Kong

First Edition
1 3 5 7 9 10 8 6 4 2

Library of Congress Cataloging in Publication Data
Monson, A. M.
Wanted: best friend / by A. M. Monson;
pictures by Lynn Munsinger.—1st ed.
p.   cm.
Summary: Cat advertises for a new playmate when
his best friend, Mouse, refuses to play checkers.
ISBN 0-8037-1483-1 (trade).—ISBN 0-8037-1485-8 (lib. bdg.)
[1. Cats—Fiction. 2. Mice—Fiction. 3. Friendship—Fiction.]
I. Munsinger, Lynn, ill. II. Title.
PZ7.M7628Wan 1997 [E]—dc20 95-22828 CIP AC

The full-color artwork was prepared using pen-and-ink and watercolor.
It was then scanner-separated and reproduced as red, blue, yellow, and black halftones.

Cat and Mouse sat at the table. They were playing
checkers. The two played the game so often that Cat
sometimes made up new rules.

"That's it," said Cat. "I won." He set up the checkers for
another game.

"That's the third time you've won," complained Mouse. "Let's play crazy eights now."

"I hate crazy eights," said Cat. "You take forever to decide which card to play."

"But when we play crazy eights, I win sometimes," said Mouse. He folded his arms across his chest. "Either we play crazy eights or I go home."

"All right," said Cat. "Go home. I'll find someone else to play with me."

"Fine," said Mouse. He picked up his hat and left.

Cat scratched his head. How would he find another
friend? Suddenly he had an idea. He grabbed a piece of
paper and a pencil. He wrote:

WANTED: BEST FRIEND
MUST LIKE TO PLAY GAMES
SEE CAT *IMMEDIATELY!*

Then he called *The Hollow Log Gazette*.

Two days later there was a knock at Cat's door.

"Did you advertise for a friend?" asked Mole.

"Yes," answered Cat. "Come in." He hoped Mole liked to play checkers as much as he did.

"How about some munchies?" asked Mole.
"Help yourself," said Cat.
Mole disappeared into the kitchen.

When he came out, he was carrying a can of soda, a jar of peanut butter, crackers, bananas, an ice cream bar, and a bag of pretzels. The can of soda tumbled to the floor. Mole kicked it toward the table.

"Ah-h," said Mole. He tossed the banana peel over his shoulder. "Now I'm ready to play."

Cat moved his checker first. Mole stuffed his mouth with crackers and peanut butter.

"Your turn," said Cat.

Mole dumped all the pretzels onto the table, then moved his playing piece.

Cat smiled. He jumped over Mole's checker using his
own. "Oh, dear," said Cat. His fingers sank into a gooey glob
of peanut butter when he touched Mole's checker.

"Time for a drink," said Mole.

"No, wait!" said Cat. But he was too late. Orange soda
sprayed from the can into Cat's face.

"This will not do," said Cat. He raced for a towel. "You cannot be a slob and be my best friend."

Cat avoided Mole's sticky fingers and led him by the arm out of the house.

He'd just finished cleaning up Mole's mess when he heard
another knock at the door.

"Did you advertise for a friend?" asked Otter. He carried a large and bumpy duffel bag.

"Yes, I did," said Cat. "Come in."

"I have everything we need to have fun," said Otter. He unzipped the bag. "Baseball, basketball, softball, football, soccer ball…"

"But I like to play checkers," said Cat. Balls bounced around his feet.

"B-or-ring!" said Otter. "These games are a lot more fun. Watch." He grabbed the basketball and tossed it into a lamp shade.

"Two points!" he yelled.

Cat raced to steady the wobbling lamp. A football sailed
past his head and through the rabbit ears on the television.

"Touchdown!" cheered Otter.

"No more," said Cat. But he was too late. Otter kicked the soccer ball into the fireplace.

"Goal!" cried Otter.

"This will not do," said Cat. He stamped out sparks. "You cannot burn my house down and be my best friend."

He made Otter pick up all the balls, then showed him to the door.

Cat was eating lunch when he heard another knock. "I do hope that's Mouse and that he's come back to play." Cat ran to the door.

"Raccoon is the name and skateboarding is my game."

"I don't know how to ride a skateboard," said Cat.

"Nothing to it," said Raccoon. He dropped two skateboards to the ground. "Get on."

"But I like to play checkers," said Cat.

"I think you're scared," said Raccoon.

"I am not," lied Cat. He closed and locked the door behind him. He put one foot on the skateboard, then the other. Raccoon gave a big push and sent Cat flying down the sidewalk.

"How do I stop?" cried Cat.

"Put your foot down," called Raccoon.

Cat didn't hear. His skateboard raced toward a busy street.

"Jump!" yelled Raccoon.
Cat closed his eyes and jumped.
CRASH! CLANG! SQUISH! Cat landed in the middle of
the neighbor's garbage.

Raccoon laughed at him.

"This will not do," said Cat. He pulled his foot out of a garbage can. "You cannot laugh at me and be my best friend." He hobbled toward home.

He plopped into his big stuffed chair. "If Mouse had a phone, I would call and invite him back." Suddenly he had an idea. He grabbed a piece of paper and a pencil. He wrote:

MOUSE
PLEASE COME BACK
WILLING TO PLAY CRAZY EIGHTS
CAT

Then he called *The Hollow Log Gazette*. Two days later there was a knock at Cat's door.

"Mouse," said Cat, "I'm so happy to see you." He led his friend to the table.

"I'm thirsty," said Mouse. He disappeared into the kitchen, then returned with a glass of water.

Cat watched Mouse set the glass on a napkin. "You're so tidy," said Cat.

"Thank you," said Mouse.

"And you never throw things around my house," said Cat.

"Wouldn't dream of it," said Mouse.

"And you don't skateboard," said Cat.

"Too dangerous for a klutz like me," answered Mouse.

Cat smiled. "Mouse," he said, "you're *my* kind of best friend."

And the two of them began to play crazy eights.

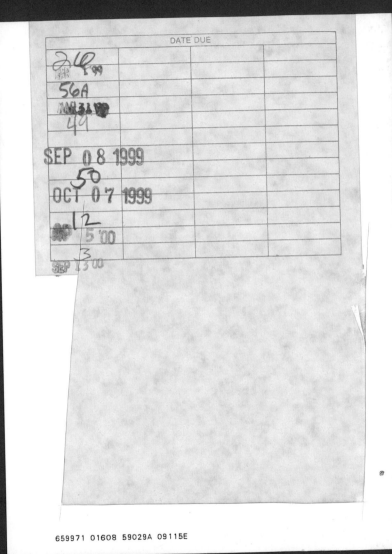

DATE DUE

FEB 24 '99			
56A			
MAR 31 '99			
49			
SEP 0 8 1999			
50			
OCT 0 7 1999			
12			
5 '00			
3			
SEP 13 '00			

659971 01608 59029A 09115E